MORE SCIENCE FICTION BY KRISTINE KATHRYN RUSCH

THE DIVING UNIVERSE

Series Reading Order

Squishy's Teams: A Diving Universe Novel

The Chase: A Diving Novel

Ivory Trees: A Diving Universe Novel

Maelstrom: A Diving Universe Novella

——— ••• ———

THE RETRIEVAL ARTIST SERIES

The Disappeared

Extremes

Consequences

Buried Deep

Paloma

Recovery Man

The Recovery Man's Bargain

Duplicate Effort

The Possession of Paavo Deshin

Anniversary Day

Blowback

A Murder of Clones

Search & Recovery

The Peyti Crisis

Vigilantes

Starbase Human

Masterminds

The Impossibles

The Retrieval Artist

———— ••• ————

STANDALONE SCIENCE FICTION NOVELS

Alien Influences

Snipers

SCIENCE FICTION COLLECTIONS

Colliding Worlds, Vol. 1

Colliding Worlds, Vol. 2

Colliding Worlds, Vol. 3

Colliding Worlds, Vol. 4

Colliding Worlds, Vol. 5

Colliding Worlds, Vol. 6

DEATH BENEFITS

A SCIENCE FICTION NOVELLA

KRISTINE KATHRYN RUSCH

CONTENTS

DEATH BENEFITS

ME

YOU SEE THEM, the shadows, everywhere. They look like the person you knew, maybe someone you were related to, maybe someone you loved. Always someone you lost.

But they aren't that someone. That's the infuriating and the comforting part. They can't be that someone. They're the right age, even though years have passed. They are too tall or too thin or too young or too old. They lack the limp or the sideways grin.

They're not quite right, but they are enough to remind you—to send that bolt of adrenaline through you, the one that says, *There he is! God, I've missed him.* And you stop and stare, or you run toward them and sometimes, the worst times, you put out a hand and call that person by the wrong name, with just a little too much hope in your voice.

Then the someone turns, and you see that you were wrong. The nose is too long, the eyes too close together, the chin too pointed. You stammer an apology and if they're kind, they say, *It's okay*, and if they're not, they angrily tell you their own name and stalk away.

The confusing ones are the ones who look at you with compassion, and then smile just a little, saying nothing as they turn their back on you and go about their business.

You want to call after those people. You want to find out who, exactly, they are, and why they looked at you like that. Could you be mistaken? Could it be the person you lost? Could it be . . .?

And you follow, but not too close, and usually you lose them in a crowd. You think: *No, no, I made a mistake, just like all the other times*, but that doubt lingers.

Sometimes it lingers just enough that you need answers, and for those answers, you—everyone—always comes to me.

KATRINA

KATRINA KLEINFELDER GOT MARRIED at sixteen because she didn't want to lose him. DeAndre Sheawn was tall and thin and had the kindest eyes she'd ever seen. He didn't stand up quite straight, and his legs were a little bowed, and she loved all of that about him.

He was six years older and he'd come into her life at the right moment. Her family's house had been half burned in a midnight carpet bombing that never should have happened—at least that was what the government had said. They had said that the city of Zelno was too far out of the war zone to suffer through any of the battles.

That was before the Etrines changed the rules, encroaching into protected territories and slaughtering anyone in their path. Total war, they'd called it, based on some historical analogy, and somehow they thought that was right.

At that point, though, Katrina—sixteen—alone, stayed in the dilapidated, water-damaged house, the one that reeked of smoke, because she thought her parents would come back from their military service and be unable to find her.

Before they left, they'd shipped her baby sister and her younger brother out of the country entirely, making them take a short shuttle to an inhabited moon at the very edge of Vorliss space where their aunt met them. Their aunt couldn't take more than two children by law, because the population inside the dome was limited.

Technically, at sixteen, Katrina was no longer a child, not according to that same law, so her parents figured she could remain at home, safe enough, with neighbors checking on her. School was nearby and had gone to year-round, partly because so many teens were in the exact same spot as Katrina—unable to leave, unable to serve, unable to completely fend for themselves.

The government was supposed to care for them, and did, more or less, with food and daily examinations at school, although the nights were terrifying, even before the bombing.

Afterwards . . .

Katrina didn't like to think about afterwards.

She only stayed in the house another week, enough to have constant flashbacks when she smelled lingering smoke. She did not let her parents know what happened, although she could have, and by rights, they could have come home, found a new place to live, and maybe figured out how to care for her.

She had gotten it into her head that they wouldn't respect her for failing to tough it out. Later, she realized that even if she had sent for them, they wouldn't have come. They were too far out. She would have been evacuated by the time they would have arrived in the neighborhood, and they would have had trouble finding her no matter what.

That night—the night of the bombing—she had helped the neighbors who had put out the fires themselves. Every neighborhood had some firefighting equipment, thanks to a farseeing watch organization, and they had used the water and the pumps and the suppressants just like they had been trained.

No one in authority had come to help; there were too many fires all over the city, in much more important neighborhoods.

So the neighbors had salvaged what they could.

Most of the neighbors left, but Katrina had nowhere to go, and what little money she had wouldn't cover travel.

The front part of the house—the living area with its large brown cushions and the kitchen with the round table that she had loved because she used it to remember better times when everyone sat around it and laughed and shared a meal—remained intact.

She slept on the largest cushion, which had somehow avoided the worst of the water, smoke, and chemicals, and ate at the table, pretending that her family was out and would return soon.

The school had been destroyed. Technically, she was supposed to receive a reassignment, but where would they send it? To her various devices? Those had stopped working because the Etrines had taken down all of the communications buildings with a single attack.

By day three, she realized she should probably walk to a different neighborhood, beg for help from another school, but she wasn't sure what direction to go in. And besides, her family wouldn't know how to find her if she moved.

She spent the entire day filled with indecision, and was about to leave when the trucks rolled in. Finally, the city's rescue workers had gotten to her neighborhood.

Finally, she met DeAndre.

He convinced her to leave. He helped her leave messages for her folks. Then, he took her to a neighborhood on the other side of the city, one he guaranteed would be safe.

And oh, it looked safe, with its intact houses and beautiful school. It didn't have a working communications array either, but there, the array was being fixed.

She moved into a house with people she didn't know and waited until she could contact her family, and

DeAndre continually checked in on her, and she didn't cling.

She was proud of herself for not clinging.

She anticipated each of his visits, though, hoping and hoping and hoping he would find her again.

He did.

And then Etrines came back. The battles—well, they weren't battles, not for her. They were days of hiding and not sleeping and whistles and explosions and dirt raining on the underground bunkers someone had built at the beginning of the war.

Then the fighting moved on. But everyone knew it would be back.

DeAndre proposed as things eased. She married him two days before he left to fight, two days she says were the best in her life, and it wasn't until later, the dreaded later, that a friend had praised DeAndre on his foresight.

No soldier thought they were going to live through this, her not-friend had said. *So he took care of you as best he could. You got his death benefits, right? The ability to travel, to leave Zelno? He's your hero.*

Her hero. Her dead hero. Because, according to the government, he was long gone.

ME

A SIGN FLOATS above my building for most to see. It includes a version of my name—Davidson Turo—in small letters beneath an ancient image of a man in a fedora looking at something through a magnifying glass.

No one here knows what a fedora is—they all call it a hat, which is technically correct—and of course, we have no need for magnifying glasses. But I love the image. It suits me, and it's memorable enough that anyone can find it.

The sign goes dim whenever the authorities are nearby. I try to remain inconspicuous. When I initially put up my sign, I deliberately put it at the very edge of Naik, back when it was small and the hub of everything on the western side of the planet. I operated illegally—still do—

which was why I figured I needed to be on the edge of things.

The city encroached and I learned that no one cared about what I did, as long as I didn't make a stink about it. The authorities did visit me once about my lack of a license, but they saw my hovel and decided pursing me for fees would cost them more than they would make, and since then, they've left me alone.

My hovel takes up the entire first floor of a building that should've been torn down a decade ago. Bugs have chewed through the original wood, which I fortified with steel, leaving the damaged wood around the steel as a kind of camouflage.

Inside, the place is strong and will last another century, provided that the conventional weapons used in the various wars fought in this sector remain conventional.

The front half, the half you would enter if you ever came to see me, is wide open, with fat steel beams that are embedded deep in the rough concrete floor. I've placed ancient and ratty furniture near tables, as well as a tiny do-it-yourself half-kitchen stocked with a dozen caffeinated beverages, some alcohol, some cannabis edibles, as well as real baked goods. Fruit and bottled water for the purists. Fortunately the system itself freshens the offerings daily, sending the proper items to compost and the rest to the nearest military shelter, half a block down.

I make a fortune at this work, so I might as well share it. That's my theory, anyway. A fortune I don't share with the authorities. I share it with those who really need it. Who needs to fund these endless wars, after all?

The other half of the main floor is hard to access. You need five codes, my eyeball print, a verbal code phrase that comes from a song my mother sang me when I was little (yes, you must sing the phrase. It cannot be recorded. Oh, and you must sound like me when doing so), and one palm print from a glove that I keep in a drawer to the door's right.

Annoying, for me anyway, since I live behind that door. I've had girlfriends tell me that the area in the back reminded them of apartments rented in the very center of some of the nearby space stations. No windows, but amenities to make up for it.

The area in the back has the full kitchen that remains stocked (same deal—recycling, composting, donating), along with an automated chef who responds quickly and without emotion to my occasionally curt orders, a lot of self-cleaning devices from the furniture to the appliances, and the ubiquitous robotic housekeeper who makes sure the sheets are fresh, the towels are fluffy, and my clothes are clean.

Those same girlfriends used to wonder if I was lonely living here, like this, with very little human contact. And I gave them all the exact same answer: *It's the best way to live.*

The relationships always ended shortly thereafter.

I didn't really care. I was more wrapped up in learning

from history, studying what-could-have-beens and searching for people hiding in plain sight. The stories I heard, they kept me going. The people I met, they made me happy I lived alone.

I believed—back then—that everything worked on its own predictable pattern.

I had a lot to learn.

MIKAH

MIKAH CRAWLEY DIDN'T MARRY and regretted it every single day of his life. He was eighteen when he and Antonio Suarez discovered each other.

They met at the hospital where Mikah was recovering from burns he'd sustained when he managed to save three little kids from a vehicle attacked by insurgents.

He didn't remember much about the rescue—most of the images in his head were from the vid feeds on the streets nearby. Single shot images rather than the moving ones, because maybe his head didn't want to deal with moving images.

First: the attack—flames shot from a blunderbuss at six vehicles traveling along a protected street. Mikah didn't look for the bad guy, didn't try to stop the illegal weapon from taking out civilians.

Instead, he saw the three kids strapped in the back of a now-burning car, their injured mother crawling out on her own, and he ran in—grabbing the metal door, using his pocket knife to undo at least one of the straps, and handing Kid One—a baby—to the woman behind him, who trotted off with it. Kid Two—a toddler (this is the famous image) clinging to his neck while he tried to grab Kid Three. He couldn't get to Kid Three without endangering Kid Two, so he handed the toddler off to another woman who took the screaming child and ran to safety.

Then he crawled inside, because he couldn't get to Kid Three through the original door.

Kid Three was squeezing herself out of the small special seat, which had frozen in place when the vehicle stopped, and she looked determined.

That was the only memory he had—the determined face, frowning as she pulled herself free. He didn't have to free her—she had done that herself, but he scooped her up, yanked her out, and handed her to someone in uniform whom, it turned out, was one of the first responders onsite —one Antonio Suarez, who took her to the waiting emergency vehicles, and then came back himself to see if he could free people from the other vehicles.

Mikah never knew how many got saved. Enough, he guessed, that this wasn't some major catastrophic event. Just the images made it to the sector-wide news because everyone loved to see rescued children.

And they were miraculously unhurt, unlike their

mother. She had suffered a broken arm, a broken collar-
bone, and a shattered hip when the vehicle stopped
suddenly, and still she tried to get to those kids. She'd
been restrained, he learned later, by some of the others
who were helping—that's what encouraged Mikah, how
many people always helped—and then he had stepped in.

Saving the day, rescuing three in a sea of losses which
had been that insurgency stage of the war.

He hadn't even registered his own pain and he
wouldn't until they put him in an emergency vehicle and
sent him to the hospital. He remembered more snatches
after that—questions, mostly—asking if the kids were all
right (they were), if their mother was going to survive (she
was), and if someone could care for those children (they
did).

He never asked who did it, never asked why, figured
he knew, and he probably did.

There were too many stories like that, too many illegal
weapons of war on the streets of Cheavis.

The government liked to pretend that Cheavis never
suffered any attacks and while that was true of organized
missions—the carpet bombs, the street-to-street fighting
so many other places had dealt with—the insurgency had
been alive and well throughout the entire war.

At least the hospitals were intact, and functioning, best
in the region because they got so many patients from all
over.

His burns were standard or so he was told and the skin

replacement easy or so he was told. The new skin itched as it grew and it never really felt like his afterwards.

He'd confessed that to Antonio when Antonio had come to visit. Apparently, Antonio was visiting everyone who survived that particular attack. Antonio, who knew who the perpetrator was and had been about to tell Mikah when Mikah had said he didn't want to know.

That caught Antonio's attention and they talked. They talked about Mikah's desire to sign up, but he couldn't— not as a citizen of Cheavis. Officially neutral, he said, which made him officially unable to help.

After you've already saved lives, Antonio had commiserated, then offered a suggestion. *I have to quit this job soon enough to go back to the front. I'm only here working instead of taking the time off the service requires. I have to go back, so why don't you train and take my place?*

Mikah thought about it. Months of forced rest with the images stuck in his head made him even more eager to do something.

So he volunteered, just another body to replace the one that was leaving.

But before Antonio left, he supervised Mikah's training, which Mikah had a clear affinity for. Along the way, Antonio noted how alone Mikah had been, and said he didn't deserve to be alone. Not a good, kind man like Mikah.

Mikah had shrugged, and Antonio had placed a hand

on his arm. *I mean it,* he had said. *I would love to end your loneliness.*

Mikah had frowned, not sure how Antonio could do that when he was leaving in less than two days.

Marry me, Antonio had said. *When I get home from the front, we'll build a life together.*

But Mikah hesitated. He'd heard too much about sudden wartime marriages, how they never worked out when the person who had been at war came home.

His response had been, *When you get home, if you still like me, we'll marry.*

And Antonio had given him a look Mikah had never seen before, something else behind Antonio's eyes, almost another person.

Mikah had a sense that Antonio felt revealed, although Mikah could never say why.

Then that look disappeared and Antonio said, *I love you, Mikah, or I wouldn't have proposed.*

Mikah had grinned to cover his own embarrassment. He had always minimized how others felt about him. He never really knew why people liked his company or why they thought he was worth their time.

But he didn't say, *I love you too.* It was expected, and at eighteen, he prided himself on not doing the expected.

Years later, he realized the expected was sometimes the best way. Sometimes the *only* way.

They parted, and Mikah was the one who did not stay in touch. He didn't want to hear about the fighting he didn't qualify for, even if most of the information was redacted.

He didn't want to see Antonio's beautiful face, sending love from an undisclosed location. The backdrops were always the same—some kind of white wall, sometimes reflecting what Mikah believed to be sunlight, sometimes gray with the crowds.

But a white wall and silence, as if nothing was happening at all.

Mikah eventually learned that the backdrop was mandated by the military and the sound, except for the voice of the person who was sending the message, scrubbed so no one would know—by imagery or sound— where that person was.

Mikah worked the medical side of the insurgency, rescuing people because he had a knack for it. He learned from Antonio how to avoid the worst injuries and how to stay on the job, even while healing.

Sometimes his new skin still itched—a phantom itch, he knew—and he remembered his first rescue, and how confused it had made him feel. In those early days, he had thought the best thing about the rescue was meeting Antonio and gaining a purpose even in the middle of an insane war.

Eventually, Mikah met the children—half grown now, exuberant, able to believe they could do anything because they had survived the worst—and he realized that no, indeed, the best thing was that he had learned how to save good and valuable lives.

He was, in a word, content—if one could be content jumping into danger at a moment's notice, seeing both the worst of humanity and its best often in the exact same second.

He had figured out his life . . . or so he thought. Because shortly thereafter, a military lawyer summoned him. Mikah expected a lawsuit from one of the rescues: sometimes people (especially perpetrators) did not want to be saved.

Instead, the lawyer told him that Antonio had been killed on the front lines and that his benefits were earmarked for Mikah.

Mikah's emotions were . . . muted. He remembered Antonio, valued what they shared, wouldn't be where he was without Antonio. But Mikah didn't exactly grieve him —not that fresh, raw grief a person had when they couldn't imagine life without the loved one. Mikah had already lived life without Antonio, for years now. Antonio was still important to him, but not in an active way.

In a historical way.

So Mikah refused the benefits, but the lawyer pushed. Antonio had no family. Even a military investigator couldn't find anyone living who was related to Antonio.

Maybe, just maybe, when Antonio had asked Mikah to marry him, maybe, just maybe, when Antonio had mentioned loneliness, he hadn't been talking about Mikah's loneliness.

Maybe, just maybe, Antonio had been talking about his own.

Which made Mikah feel guilty. He had been about to refuse a second time when he thought to ask what would happen to the benefits if no one claimed them.

Why, they'd get absorbed back into the system, the military lawyer had said, as if everyone knew that.

To be used how? Mikah had asked.

However the government sees fit, the lawyer had said. *Undesignated funds*.

Undesignated. Mikah was fighting undesignated funds already. Those funds were why he had to pull people out of burning vehicles, why he had to carefully pick apart destroyed buildings to see if there were bodies inside, why he had to hold sobbing children who had just watched a parent die.

That meant Mikah had no decision to make at all. He took the benefits, even though they made him feel like some kind of fraud.

He hadn't said *I love you*, although his relationship with Antonio was the closest thing he had come to love; he hadn't said yes to marriage; he wondered whenever the rather startling amount of money hit his account every month if he had hurt Antonio badly, Antonio who had loved him and whom Mikah now knew, he had never really loved.

Not in those grand passions that inspired stories or lifelong relationships, that led to children and an imagined future and comforting each other through the best and worst.

Mikah had never met anyone like that, wasn't sure if he was capable of feeling that way about anyone.

But Mikah wanted to rewind time. He wanted to go back to that proposal and be a stronger, wiser human. If he could go back, he would have said, *Find someone to love you with all their heart. You deserve it more than anyone. You are the best person I've ever met.*

He had never said that either.

So he tried to be the best person ever, not that he could. Not like Antonio, whose heart Mikah had broken. Antonio, whom Mikah thought about every single day, and wished, somehow, that he could do it all over again.

ME

SHE CAME to my office because I make everyone come to my office. I have to see them because I constantly deal with fake people, so I need to know if the person I'm working for is real.

She had to get past my front door, which has a government-issued sensor that matches her biometrics to her built-in identification. And, no, I did not get that sensor from the government itself. I have a lot of hidden tech in this place, mostly to verify identities, and much of that tech is illegal.

She was a thin woman, naturally thin, no bones showing beneath the skin. And tall as well, with only a few expected curves front and back. Her short hair was auburn, which was probably natural, given the rest of her coloring—the pale freckled skin, the auburn-brown eyes, the slight auburn color to the fine hairs on her arms.

She wore a short-sleeved tunic, silver and gray, over matching pants, and flat shoes, and she carried some kind of clutch purse in her right hand, tucking it against her hip as if she were trying to keep it invisible.

The clutch purse wasn't invisible to my sensors. There were a few coins inside as well as some tiny storage devices. There was also an ancient handheld device tucked into its own case.

What was invisible to my sensors, and to my eyes initially, was that she wasn't as young as she seemed when she stood outside the building.

As she came all the way inside, and the harsh bright white lights that I kept near the door caught her face, I noticed fine lines near her eyes and mouth, lines that would become grooves if she let them.

Her mouth had a permanent downturn. Something about her had an air of perpetual sadness, as if she had never seen a moment of happiness in her entire life.

I had seen her approach and had been monitoring her since she crossed the street toward my door. She hadn't contacted me ahead of time, so this visit seemed spontaneous, even though I knew it wasn't.

The ancient handheld in the clutch would have told me that, even if I hadn't seen her lingering nearby for the past month, her height and thinness making her conspicuous, no matter what crowd she was in.

She saw me, leaning against a table in the center of the room, and she stopped walking. Not because I was large or muscular or intimidating.

I'm as inconspicuous as my office, my edges just as chewed, my interior filled with more steel than I ever allowed in this place. Not real steel, but metaphorical steel.

I'm hard to budge and even harder to bend.

Most people don't even see me when they first come in, but she had, which made her unusual from the start.

"Davidson Turo?" she asked, her voice shaking.

If I moved wrong, she would bolt.

I moved my head once, up and down ever so slightly, not quite a nod, but enough of an acknowledgement that it made her frown. The movement added even more fine lines and potential wrinkles to that face.

"I'm Jessica O'Shea," she said, as if I should know the name. "I understand that you verify people?"

That's what they called it, the clients. In their ratings and rankings, based on the perpetual need for some kind of organization in a disorganized world, someone—an old client maybe—had listed me under Investigators, and added the phrase People Verifier.

The reviews clarified just enough and for a time, brought me too many unnecessary clients. I weathered them, learned to figure out the difference between the curiosity seekers, the lazy, and the people truly in pain.

"I wouldn't call it that," I said to her. "I don't verify anyone."

"But your ad—"

"I don't advertise," I said.

"But I saw—"

"Information put up by people not me," I said.

I've had versions of this conversation dozens of times, maybe even hundreds of times, and it always seems to fluster the client. It was no different for Jessica O'Shea. She shifted, looked at the door as if it had forced her to make a mistake, and seemed like she was going to turn around, leave without telling me who or what she needed verified.

Which was fine with me. I didn't need the work and I had long since lost my curiosity about the minutiae of other people's problems.

"So what *do* you do?" she asked, turning back toward me. A slight red color infused her freckled cheeks, color that had come up from her too-long neck.

"Mostly, I shatter dreams," I said. The script, which I was staying on, had been honed over a decade or more. I did shatter dreams and I wanted people to know about that from the start.

"Which means what?" She hadn't moved from her place near the door, but her body had grown tense, rigid, as if her entire self was already resisting what I was going to tell her.

This was the tough part of the script. A decade of

perpetual war all over the sector meant lots of dead, people who left without saying goodbye. The war had cooled enough that for two years, the authorities were declaring what we were living through a peace, even though it wasn't, not really.

Attacks weren't huge anymore. Cities were doing well throughout the sector. Flare-ups usually happened in tight quarters—space stations, barely inhabited moons, the occasional skirmish between smaller ships.

Here, the war was essentially over. On the most habitable parts of Vorless, where the cities were, people had started to rebuild. Rebuilding meant reassessing. For some, rebuilding meant attempting to recreate all that had been lost.

"So," I said, "what does shattering dreams mean?"

I chose my words carefully. This was the part of the speech that usually made people leave. They had come thinking I was a conventional investigator, one who would track down someone who was missing or expend incredible resources trying to find out what was often behind the vague killed-in-action notices so many people had received.

"It means," I said, "that you've come here because you thought you've seen someone you lost."

She raised her chin at my first sentence, which led me to believe she had researched me. It would have surprised me if she hadn't, given that she had been hovering outside for nearly a month.

I tried not to let the speech sound rote. "You'll describe the person you lost, give me information about them, and then tell me where you thought you saw them. I will investigate as best I can. More often than not, I will discover things you will not like."

I kept it vague because there was no need to be harsh at this stage.

Except, apparently, for Jessica O'Shea.

"What wouldn't I like?" she asked, that chin even higher.

If she pushed too hard, she would force me to say the words I didn't want to say. She would not like the fact that she really hadn't seen her loved one, that she was chasing ghosts because chasing a ghost was easier than believing someone once so vital, once so important, was actually gone.

Her chin was up in that challenge, her eyes hooded, her body so tense I thought she might snap in half.

I had a hunch she wouldn't like anything I told her.

"It depends on how you lost the person you're searching for," I said, still relying on the speech. "If I need to, I'll verify government information, and that will tell me if the phantom you saw in this city is actually the person you're searching for."

"How do you know I saw someone here?" she asked. Fortunately, I had distracted her.

"Why else come to me?" I asked in return.

"You're the only one who does this work," she said.

Which wasn't true. There were others, scattered all over Vorless. They did something similar, but called it by other names. Some of those people were brilliant scam artists, working in concert with folks who could change their appearance enough to be convincing. Some could lead their victims on using holos and fake images. Just enough to make the victim feel like they had seen their loved one. Others who did this work were as legitimate as I was, using similar tools to do similar investigations.

"I'm not the only one," I said. "If you had seen your phantom in another city, you would have gone to someone there."

Her eyes narrowed as she assessed me.

I added another sentence that often made people leave. "You should know," I said, "that I confine my work to Naik."

Which led to the misapprehension that I was the only one who did this work here. The scam artists were everywhere, and they did not make my job easier.

Nor did Naik herself, which had been a hub of clandestine activity after the initial fighting moved on.

"If you're searching for someone in a different city," I said, "I can give you the names of a legitimate operator there."

She stared at me. I felt it, that tug inside her. Part of her wanted to leave now. That feeling, though, was coming from her loss and her unwillingness to have a dream shattered.

The dream was simple: maybe her loved one was alive out there, living without her. Maybe that person had even forgotten her, some kind of injury had destroyed an important memory center.

Such things rarely happened, but the culture had come to accept the myth, particularly in some popular entertainments. That myth fed the scam artists, who, in turn, made sure the stories of their "solutions" made their way back into the media.

It was so convenient—assuming that someone had forgotten due to medical reasons. It explained why that living person had not come home, and it would explain personality differences, things that no matter how much research a scammer did, they would never get entirely right.

I'd seen the look she wore dozens of times on the faces of many different clients. That client would weigh me, seeing my insignificant little self, my harsh words, the fact that this person might discover that yes, indeed, their loved one was dead.

So many potential clients fled right here, and I welcomed that. I did not want to deal with illusions and shattered hopes. It was my least favorite part of the job.

She brought her clutch up, and opened it, and as she did so, the moment passed. She had committed to this path, whatever it was.

Before she even put her hand in the clutch, I knew what she was going to remove. It would be the ancient handheld, and it would hold images and memories and all of those hopes and dreams wrapped into one.

This part of the work always took a while. I had to be half therapist half investigator. I'd have to tease out information about old relationships. I would have to find the reality scattered among the lies that we all tell ourselves about our lives.

It was a delicate process, one that would lead to the success or failure of the investigation—regardless of whether or not we discovered if the supposed phantom was real.

"Let's sit," I said.

She frowned at me, her hand still hovering near that clutch.

"This will take time," I said, as if I hadn't seen her hesitation. "We might as well be comfortable."

She swallowed visibly, hand inside that clutch now. I had confused her with the offer because she was so set on proving to me that her loved one existed.

I didn't want for some kind of assent from her. Instead, I led her to the most comfortable of my ancient furniture groupings. This one was close to the wall, and had a lot of soft lighting. There were three couches, which formed a sort of fort, and a love seat with its back to the entire room. Tables on wheels let the client put something on a surface, and then that something could get pushed toward me, without either of us standing at all.

I didn't like to get too physically close to these people.

They were all broken in some way, and sometimes that brokenness wasn't evident. Sometimes they didn't show any evidence of the brokenness until I got too close, and then they would push me away or scream and flee or lash out with fists and kicks.

Sometimes those fists and kicks were trained, and I'd get more than bruised.

So I set up far from the client to protect myself.

I had also made sure there was recording tech in the walls, so that I would have a record of this entire meeting. The tables could pull information from most devices and could also make copies of any paper that was placed on it.

Most of the information I collected would get trashed after a few weeks, when it became clear that the client was no longer interested. Sometimes I used the information as I had originally intended, as part of the investigation that I would get paid much too much to finish.

Occasionally, the information got used as a threat—not by me, never by me initially, anyway—but it always started out as if I had done something wrong. Some client might threaten me, threaten to bring in the authorities, and I would remind them that they had been culpable. I would show them evidence of their threats.

Twice, I had used the imagery as a cudgel to extort money, usually from a lawyer representing the possible client, the one who had assaulted me despite my precautions.

So I wasn't nervous sitting here, but I wasn't comfortable either. In addition to the furniture and the rolling tables, I had a laser pistol under the cushion and an electrified truncheon, which I had used more than once.

I did not sit until she arrived at the grouping. I stood in front of the oldest, rattiest couch. The cushions on top sagged uninvitingly. They were a strange grayish greenish color that clearly was a faded version of the original.

Her choices would be the couch to my left, the couch opposite me, or the loveseat. By hovering close to the left arm of my couch, I silently deterred most people from ever sitting on the couch pushed against the wall.

Those that did sit there were usually needy or clingers or people who loved to get too close and intimidate.

She chose to sit directly across from me. The benefits of that couch—at least to the naked eye—were that it seemed newer. The cushions were thick and the couch was a uniform brushed gold, just like it had been designed.

That couch had been completely rebuilt. It had restraints that could hold someone back who wanted to lunge across the table. It could record biometrics. It had a back-up audio recording system as well.

It was the most complicated couch, but the others had some systems built in as well. I learn from my mistakes. I work alone, so I protect myself as best I can, which is often very well.

I fail less now than I used to.

She glanced around as if she could see any traps I set

up. Apparently she didn't notice any because she sat as I sat.

She pulled the handheld out of her clutch and set both on the table before her. The handheld was still inside its case. If the case was any indication, the unit was prewar, which meant it was probably on its last legs.

"I don't want to look at images yet," I said. "I want to know exactly why you're here."

Her hand hovered over the handheld for a moment, as if I had derailed her and the message hadn't yet gotten to her fingers.

Then she nodded.

"This might take a while," she said.

"That's all right," I said. "It usually does."

OLLIE

AT FIRST, all Ollie White could discuss was his embarrassment. He wouldn't tell people how it started. He didn't want them to know because he was a private man who had—in his words—lived too long.

The meeting happened—he thought—accidentally. Later, he wasn't sure if that was the case. Later, he wasn't sure of anything, and even that fact embarrassed him.

He'd been in his usual coffee shop on Austin Station. He'd moved to the station because it held no memories for him. He'd seen promotions for a senior-living center on the Station—complete with an apartment and elder care when and if he should need it.

By then, he was completely alone and terrified of that fact. He'd been searching for some place to go. He hadn't even considered a space station, until a blizzard in his seventieth year kept him confined to the house for two weeks, and he nearly ran out of food.

He'd tell the story to new friends—he'd always had a reputation as a raconteur—and he'd laugh about it, about the growing arthritis, the way the cold had turned his fingers numb, the fact that he'd had to cook what meals he could scrounge on the meals-prep device his son had brought home from one of his tours and left in Ollie's basement.

Ollie had stared at the snow piling outside his window, listened to the wind whipping around a house that had barely survived the groundquakes from attacks miles from him, and figured he could let it end there or he could give himself one last adventure.

The promotions for space station living had shown up right after, as the snow was melting and the news predicted more within the next two weeks.

There had been more, and he'd weathered them, but he'd also managed to sell his house and 90% of his memories. They weighed him down, he said when he told the story after he first arrived on Austin Station, and what he didn't say was that he missed them so very much.

He hadn't expected to. He had expected to feel relief.

The rooms he'd paid for with half of his life savings were bland and colorless, his view was of stars in the distance, sure, and it was exciting to see space ships of different types go by on the way to the docking ring, but it was claustrophobic. At least he'd had the foresight to buy a unit with retractable shelves, so that should a sudden loss of gravity happen, the shelves would recede into the walls, taking the old books and knickknacks he loved into a protected space so they wouldn't break.

He had initially followed the suggestions made by the senior living council and posted images of the past on his walls, but he took those down within the first few days, going for the generic waterfalls and multicolored sunsets —eventually taking those down too because they made him sad.

Everything made him sad, except the coffee shop which was a hefty hike from his place, outside of the senior living zone. He'd spend too much of his daily allowance there, sipping everything from the crap they called black coffee to an ice-cream mocha that had too many calories and always gave him a brown-and-white mustache that made him look like a child who had never learned how to wipe off his face.

He'd sit in the corner, and look out the windows at people passing on the promenade, and the day that an entire unit of soldiers went through in their parade golds, smiling and marching and barely able to contain their excitement at being off their training vessel—well, that day, he had lost the tenuous hold he had on his emotions and sobbed so hard that three other patrons wanted to call the medics and the woman who owned the place had stopped them.

She sat beside him, patting his back ineffectually,

when another man—mid-thirties maybe, black hair trimmed within an inch of its life, brown skin so smooth that he'd gone above and beyond regulations to make sure he had no errant facial hair—leaned over both of them.

I have this, Molly, he'd said gently, and pulled a chair a tad too close to Ollie. The man was wearing a blue-and-gold uniform—mid-range officer, one who didn't have a lot of command, not yet. His shoes, which were what Ollie could see most clearly, were spit-shined. They hadn't been off the station yet—or maybe not out of the space ship.

Not a ground troop, then, not someone who served on real land, like Ollie had decades before. Like his son had, before . . .

The man handed him a cloth napkin, probably offered by Molly, and Ollie took it, sobbing into it, trying to keep his voice down.

He was crying and embarrassed that he was crying and unable to do anything about any of it. He couldn't even tell the nice soldier man to go the hell away, which he wanted to do, so that he could sob in peace.

He finally gulped some air, managed to catch himself, and tried to wave the man away. But the man either didn't understand or pretended not to understand.

"The cadets are happy," the man said in a low tone. "Their first R n R after graduation."

Ollie nodded.

"And that makes you sad," the man said. It wasn't a

question. It didn't even require a response, so Ollie didn't give him one.

Ollie's mind was trying to skip past the vid his son had sent of a similar moment at the end of training, all the joy and laughter on all of those young faces who had no damn idea what faced them in the early years of the war.

Or hell, the later years, if any of them survived that long. Some of them had.

His son had. Kinda. For a while. Enough to come home and prove that the joyful little boy that Ollie had raised was gone forever. Joy was not a concept that had any place in this universe.

Ollie might've said that out loud.

And the man before him gave him a small, sad smile. "There's always room for joy," he said. "Even if it's fleeting. There's always room for joy."

Ollie had shaken his head. He couldn't imagine joy any longer.

But the man—who introduced himself as Ajani Sayer —said, "Give me tomorrow. I will show you joy."

It sounded like a con. Ollie vowed not to go, but when the following morning dawned, he found himself at the coffee shop where he had embarrassed the heck out of himself. He planned to linger near the door, see if Ajani had bothered to show.

He had. He had already ordered Ollie's iced mocha, but in a carry-all cup with a reusable straw and a solid lid.

Ollie took it, even though the cold hurt his arthritic

fingers, and did not sit down at the table. He had a speech planned—one that would thank Ajani and would make sure that they never had to see each other again.

But Ollie couldn't get the words out of his mouth.

Are you ready? Ajani had asked, and Ollie had held up a single finger, asking Ajani to wait. Ollie went to the counter, got a holder for the cup so that the chill wouldn't touch his hand any longer, and then followed Ajani out the door.

They went down two levels, to hydroponics, which Ollie had always avoided. This was the working part of the station, and he respected work; he didn't want to interrupt those who did it.

Ajani did not seem to have those qualms. He walked with purpose past doors that had writing in several languages that Ollie couldn't read. The one word he could read was *visitors*, which surprised him. There was even an arrow that matched the color of the word, pointing those visitors in a specific direction.

Ajani opened an opaqued door, and as he did, humid warmth wafted out, bringing with it the smell of early spring. Loam, and new greenery, and the hint of flowers.

Ollie had never been able to separate the flower scents—except roses and lilies, which were always too strong. The scents here were a lot more delicate, almost hesitant, which made him think of cold rains and sunny days.

Ajani held the door for Ollie, who wasn't sure he

wanted to walk inside. He wasn't sure he wanted the memories.

But Ajani raised his eyebrows, and Ollie stepped in, to discover a garden of a type he'd only seen in images. Green vines with white flowers on arbors. More ropy vines overhead with purple flowers draping down. A carpet of moss that led straight. A carpet of grass went to his right. A carpet of blue flowers cropped close to the surface went to his left.

Ajani didn't choose any of those directions, though. He waved a hand, saying, *There are benches and water-falls and misters and artificial sunlight ahead. But I wanted to show you one thing.*

He crouched near a sapling and opened a small carved container that looked like it was made of wood. Of course it wasn't made of wood. Wood was something people brought here or replicated here because it was too expen-sive to cut and tend.

Inside the container was a small stone, polished and warm. Ajani pulled it out, and said, *It's a token. It will allow you to qualify to take a plant back to your quarters.*

Qualify? Ollie asked.

You have to prove that you won't kill it. Ajani said.

Ollie had no idea if he would kill a plant. He had never tended a plant. His wife had done so, but she was long gone and he had never asked her how, nor had he ever cared to try.

Ajani led Ollie on a fake stone path that glittered in the

filtered light. It looked like dappled sunlight pouring down through trees. The trees were real, but the sunlight couldn't be.

They reached a small glass wall, with a door half open. Ajani pulled it open all the way and a bell tinkled. A woman, as old as Ollie if her papery skin was any indication, greeted Ajani by name.

I'd like to show my friend the container gardens, Ajani had said, and she had told him to go ahead.

Ajani led Ollie through shelves covered with supplies labeled mulch and soil and seeds. The loamy smell grew here, and the lighting changed with each section. Sometimes it was dim, and sometimes it was tinted with blue and sometimes it was a warm reddish yellow.

They reached the back of this strange room, and there, on the floor and on several open shelves, were long containers, each with different items inside. Some had a morass of flowers, from yellow to orange to pink. Others had herbs, whose different leaves he recognized because his wife once had a tiny herb garden to assist her with cooking.

The container gardens were too big for him, too complicated. He could barely take them in, and what he could take in brought back the wrong kind of memory. There was no joy here. There was only twisted pain from moments he wanted to forget.

Ajani studied his face, and then said, *Let's start small.*

He led Ollie to a single tall shelf stuck in a corner,

bathed in golden light. On each individual shelf were pots, larger ones on the lower shelves, but on the shelf directly in front of him were pots not much bigger than his thumb. Each pot held a bit of greenery and a bit of bloom. He actually recognized the plants. Violets, which ironically came in many colors, as his wife—also a Violet—told him with a laugh.

I'm not purple, she had said, *and neither are all of these. Some are pink and blue . . .*

. . . and actual violet, he whispered, his eyes moist. He hadn't let himself miss her, because his son had left on another tour at the very same time.

I didn't quite hear that, Ajani said, and Ollie shook his head. He reached for one of the tiny pots. The pot itself was some kind of ceramic (or fake ceramic) that someone had painstakingly painted with green and gold tendrils. The violets seemed to grow out of that, although he saw a thumbnail's worth of soil.

He wanted that one. He hadn't wanted anything on this silly station before, not to take back to his room, but he wanted that tiny pot with its little teeny plant. He could care for that, because he already did.

How do I buy this? he asked Ajani.

Take the token and give it to Marjorie, because here, the first one is always free.

First one. Ollie didn't want another. He wanted this one. He ignored that last comment from Ajani and threaded his way past more single pots with different kinds of flowers spilling out of them. White and gold and orange flowers, types he didn't recognize. Some plants that looked more like bulbous fingers to him, and some that seemed dangerous with little spikes on their flat green leaves.

He avoided them, set the pot on the desk near the woman—Marjorie, apparently—and handed her the token.

Do you know how to care for it? she asked.

He almost shook his head, but then he remembered Violet—his Violet—admonishing him to care for her violets.

They like humidity, she had said, *damp soil—not wet soil—and bright, filtered light, so don't move them.*

He repeated those instructions to Marjorie who smiled, her paper cheeks cascading into tiny wrinkles.

Yes, she said, *but they also like company and conversation. So talk to it and bring me images of it, almost every day, because at some point, you'll have to move it to a new pot.*

An hour before that sentence would have upset him, would have moved him to another part of the store without the tiny violet. But he was ready for this now, something had changed.

Maybe it was that small moment of joy.

Later, weeks later, after he'd actually invited Marjorie to his tiny abode to help him move the violets to a slightly larger pot, he bought Ajani coffee, and asked, *How did you know that would cheer me up?*

I didn't, Ajani said, *but people who come from land usually like that part of hydroponics.*

And Ollie did. Just like he liked coffee with Ajani and the occasional conversation with Marjorie. And slowly, Ollie realized he had made the right choice to come here after all.

He told that to Ajani the week before Ajani was redeployed. He was going to go with those green troops somewhere terrifying, and, Ollie knew, would probably never come back.

I wish you didn't have to go, Ollie said. *I will miss you.*

I will miss you too, Ajani said, *but you'll remember me every time you go to hydroponics.*

And Ollie did remember him there. And remembered his wife when he looked at the violets. And slowly, ever so slowly, got up enough courage to look at the documents the government had sent about his son.

There were benefits in those documents that Ollie had never taken. He did now, so he could set up a memorial in the garden, because hydroponics allowed for that, a little plaque on a pretty rock or, in the case of Ollie and his son, a bench near one of the fountains, a place that looked just a little bit like a park they used to go to when Ollie's boy was young.

Eventually, there was more money. Ajani did not return, and his death—well, Ollie didn't look up Ajani's death, even though everyone in the little hydroponics community could have. They were—or rather the gardens were—the recipients of Ajani's death benefits, since he had no family.

The designation that came with the benefits was simple: *Share a little joy*.

It was an admonition the tiny community took to heart.

Ollie didn't set up a memorial for Ajani. Marjorie did that. She did not take the money from the death benefits, though. She used that money for more plants and pots and artists to decorate them. Instead, she collected funds for the memorial. Ollie donated to it. He also made a virtual comment that people could view if they wanted, talking about Ajani's recipe for a little bit of joy.

Eventually, Ollie gave short in-person presentations, because people liked hearing from him. It astonished him, that these little lessons he had learned from Ajani inspired so many people.

Ollie did not take credit for anything he said. Instead, he talked about Ajani, and always started with his embarrassment. *It took a better man than I am to see my pain and not judge*, Ollie would say. *And I find myself forever grateful*.

ME

JESSICA O'SHEA PUT the ancient handheld on the table between us and went through her memories. Most people started with images, but she didn't. Instead, she started with their meeting, which was like other meetings I'd heard about over the years—a smile, an awkward conversation, the brush of a hand, a spark of attraction—that moment, that indefinable moment, when two people knew they had something in common, but they didn't know what.

Their first meeting happened years ago, but not prewar like I thought because of the handheld. Back when the coastal city of Saanu was blockaded. Supplies like food and water were airlifted in, but nothing else. Whatever was there remained there for nearly a year.

People used old tech. They wore old clothes. They made do with worn out dishes and tools. They survived.

O'Shea had found the handheld, and it had worked, much to her lover's dismay. He had predicted it wouldn't, and he said he wanted nothing to do with it.

That was when she showed me the first image she took with the handheld—a crackling and somewhat destroyed holo of a man reaching for the device, protesting faintly that there was no point in saving images on that thing, since they would vanish and not be recovered.

I could barely see his face, caught the edges of his cheeks and a very short haircut. His hand—wide and dark, except the palm, which was lighter—grabbed and then smothered the image altogether.

"And that," I said, making it a question, even though it really wasn't, "is Keenan?"

"Yes." Her voice wobbled. She really didn't look at the holo. I'd seen that before with possible clients as well. They didn't see the images; they saw the memories.

I stared at the outline of his face, hating the sense that I had, the sense of something familiar. That happened to me sometimes, particularly with partial images. A trick of the light, a hint of movement, the shadows from the backdrop often led me to misinterpret something.

It was a common problem, a human problem, something I tried to explain to my clients and potential clients. The brain took pieces of images and tried to put them in context. That context usually started with the familiar and, if the unwary let it, would stay there.

I am not unwary. If anything I am too wary. I never let that feeling of familiarity overwhelm me. Instead, I acknowledge it, and I move past it.

Which was what I did in that moment.

I did not frown. I did not change my expression at all. Instead, I asked, as calmly as I could, "Do you have a better image?"

She didn't even look up at me. She was still studying that holo, or rather, not quite studying it. Reliving the memory.

"Yes," she said quietly. "I have a lot of images."

It took her a moment—she clearly did not want that holo to disappear, even though it would someday. The device was old and the holo was losing its cohesiveness. I wondered if she knew that at some point, she would never be able to call it up again.

If she did become my client, and if I liked her at the end of our working relationship, I would let her know that my table had just made a copy of that holo.

She picked up the handheld and squeezed it. The holo vanished. She flicked something on the side, and several images appeared, flat and tiny.

I had forgotten the features of these handhelds. Not everything immediately turned into a holo, because the handheld did not have the capacity for that. You had to choose if you wanted the image to blow up into a holo or not.

"May I?" I asked, extending my hand.

She frowned at my fingers for a moment, clearly not wanting anyone else to touch her device.

She half-handed it to me, then stopped, then her lips thinned. "I—um . . . what do you need to see?"

She wasn't going to let me touch it. She was still that deeply in love with Keenan and she was also deep in mourning.

Those were two good facts for me to know, because emotions clouded memory. She *wanted* to see Keenan again, so a fleeting glance, a half-seen movement, might become—to her mind—the man himself.

"Give me ten," I said, "from the earliest to the most recent."

She took the handheld back, and scrolled through the images. I saw them as a blur of color, floating about her fingers. Finally, she stopped and pressed one.

A holo floated up, a little slower than modern holos, and with a bit of a sparkle and crackle. Then a man slept above my table. Beneath him, there was the hint of a cushion on the ground or a couch, not a bed, because whatever he was on was shorter than he was.

A blanket covered his torso, but what I could see of it was lean and muscular. His face was turned slightly upward, eyes closed, lashes long enough to grace the top of his cheeks. His hair was tightly cropped against his skull.

The skin from his neck upward was darker than the skin of his chest. He had clearly gotten a lot of sunlight and had not protected himself from it. One hand gripped the side of the blanket; the other was lost in its fold.

This was an image a lover would surreptitiously take, their beloved at their most vulnerable.

The man in the holo seemed deceptively young, his dark face smooth, but his neck older, with crepelike wrinkles around his Adam's apple, suggesting that he had allowed himself to have some work done on his appearance.

"What else?" I asked.

She showed me several, none of them posed. Keenan with his hand up, turning away from the lens. Keenan walking away, but looking over his shoulder—not smiling or even approving. Keenan, from a distance, head bent, looking like a man working on yet another device.

That sense of familiarity continued, and it nagged at me. The more holos I saw, the more I realized I *had* seen this man before, but I could not put him in any context.

All I knew was that I hadn't left Naik in more than a decade. If I had seen Keenan elsewhere, it would have been a long time ago, and our interaction would have had to have been memorable enough to survive in my mind for all those years.

However, had I seen him around Naik, especially recently, he would have been a shadow, a shade, in my consciousness, one of those people we all see, sometimes daily, who are as much a part of our world as the buildings, the streets, and the air around us. Just as significant too—we need them, but they are not something we concentrate on.

Maybe something crossed my face, because O'Shea said, "What are you seeing?"

I usually don't let my clients see my reactions, but rarely do I have the same sense of familiarity that my clients bring to me.

"Do you have other images?" I asked. "Ones he posed for?"

She frowned. "He didn't like images," she said. "He said that they weren't real and they interfered with memories."

And they could be used to trace someone, from their body style and movements to their face.

She was watching me a bit too closely.

"Is that a problem?" she asked.

I shook my head. "Candid images are best," I said. "But sometimes portraits, especially those done by professionals, capture the personality."

"You don't need something like that for his personality," she said. "I can tell you about that."

"I'm sure you can," I said, "but that would require me to get to know you better so that I can filter out your perceptions. Sometimes images tell me just as much."

She shifted on that couch, clearly bristling at my words. "You're saying I didn't know him?"

"Not at all," I said. "But everyone is multifaceted. The person he was with you is not the person he was when he was . . . say . . . at work. Just like you're not the person you were with him when you're here with me."

She made a small noise in the back of her throat. I couldn't tell if the sound was agreement, disagreement, or one of those noises people made when they wanted the person they were speaking with to think they were paying attention when they really weren't.

"How did he die?" I asked, mostly to distract her from the images.

Her gaze met mine, steady and steely.

"He didn't," she said.

RUSSELL

RUSSELL VONG FORMED a business to make personal death notices after his brother died. He was inspired by the callousness of the military. They didn't seem to care how they informed families of their loss.

The Vong family received their notification of the death of Ray Vong through three different forms of communication, none of them with an actual human being attached.

The notifications had the blandest of information. There were two dates: the date the notification was sent and the date his brother died. The rest of it was painfully sparse:

We have been requested to inform you of the death of Ray Vong. Ray Vong's death happened during the defense of the city of Cheavis. Images of the body, already identi-

fied by the officer in charge, as well as testimony of those involved in the military action, can be provided upon request. Due to circumstances on the ground, his body is unavailable for return.

Ray Vong listed you as the recipient of his survivor benefits. To access them, contact . . .

There wasn't even a contact name. Just six different methods of communicating with the death benefits offices, scattered around Vorless. Fortunately, that procedure was relatively smooth, which had surprised everyone in the family except Russell's mother. She believed the procedure was smooth because so many people were dying in these endless wars, and no one in the family contradicted her.

The death benefits didn't concern Russell. The benefits went to his mother, who found them small consolation. Instead, she wanted to know how her son had died, whether he was in pain, whether or not he lingered, and if he had someone he cared about beside him when he died.

All unanswerable questions, lost in the bureaucracy. Russell's remaining brother, Roy, decided to brave the bureaucracy to find the answers. He plunged into documentation, interviews, and many many many conversations with the military brass, mostly finding out nothing.

The mission had been classified. According to the military, no one got information about anything connected to the defense of Cheavis.

But Russell continued to turn the notification over and

over and over again in his mind, as if he were toying with the sharp edge of a broken tooth. His mother might not have obsessed about her boy's last days if she had known more about the circumstances of his death when it occurred.

Russell couldn't help his mother—no one could, really —but he felt that no other family should go through the same pain. He volunteered to help in the notification office, but they turned him down.

He wasn't military.

But, one of the officials who worked there told him, *we do partner with private firms on various projects. Right now, there is no one to handle death notifications.*

Death notifications were seen as a bureaucratic necessity, straightforward and easy to do. Apparently, no one in any of the services thought about the end result, the families who were learning that they would never see their loved ones again.

That callousness had to stop.

It took Russell three years to develop his company, and another year to get the military to partner with him. His company became a clearing house. Soldiers could sign up to have their death notifications go through the clearing house, and the clearing house would guarantee that someone empathetic would make a personal notification after discovering a few details about the death. The personal notification would include instructions on how to apply for death benefits, should the government fail to send that information to the survivors.

After the company was running well on its own, Russell made sure that he spent at least three days per month doing notifications himself. He had to stay on top of the policies and procedures. At first, he made his staff do as many notifications as they could fit into their daily schedule, and then he realized after he had done his three days, that he had been prioritizing work over empathy.

He changed the company policy to no more than two notifications per day. The staff always paired up, and the primary on the first notification was never the primary on the second. That way, one of the responders was fresh enough to handle the emotions that would come directly at them.

People were unpredictable in their responses, slamming doors, screaming in disbelief, asking with a trembling voice if the notification was about their loved one, or bursting into tears before a single word was spoken.

Over the years, Russell had ducked fists and cradled the hopelessly bereaved. He had ferried the emotionally fragile to hospitals. He had stayed on premise until someone else—someone connected to the survivor—could arrive.

Finally, he added a secondary service, one his own people could contact, that would arrive shortly after the personal notification occurred, so that the survivors would get emotional support and whatever else they needed physically to make it through this impossible time.

His business was compassion, and he was the best at it he could possibly be.

But it wore on him.

One night, after completing his monthly stint of notifications, he found himself on a park bench near a lake that glistened in the sunlight. He wasn't quite sure how he had gotten there—he had stopped after leaving the last grieving couple who seemed to believe that reining in emotions was the best way to deal with bad news.

His partner had gone back to the office, believing that the last notification had been easy. It hadn't been. The repressed bothered Russell more than those whose emotions were on the surface.

He was always afraid that the repressed would become casualties themselves, and he was unable to find a way to help them with their grief. No program he could come up with, no counselors he talked to, could figure out how to kickstart healing.

He had begun to see the repressed as the walking dead. They might continue with their lives, but it would be without joy or warmth or any sort of living whatsoever.

He knew that, figuratively, the repressed would die at the moment of notification, and there was nothing he could do about it.

That particular day had seemed worse than the usual notification of the repressed. The air had felt pregnant with unexpressed grief, and he had found himself shaking when he left. His partner had placed a hand on his arm, offering to take him back to the office, but he had refused. He knew he needed to walk. When he saw a patch of green ahead, he stopped. From the entry to the park, he could see the sparkling water, and it spoke to him of a tranquility which, he realized, he desperately needed.

He walked toward the tranquility, the air fresh and clean, the sun warm, and slowly the shaking stopped.

Until he saw a man sitting on a green park bench, head flung back, eyes closed. One arm draped over the chair's iron railing as if the man had been dropped there.

Russell straightened. The man was dead or injured. Russell couldn't fall apart at this moment, because the man needed him.

Which, Russell knew, was ironic, because the situation was forcing him to repress his feelings—at least for the time being.

His feet crunched slightly on the dry grass, and the man sat up, startling Russell so much that he let out a small eep of surprise.

The man turned around.

He had a long face with dark eyes, curly black hair and an expression that Russell recognized. Hopelessness.

Grief.

Russell continued walking toward the bench.

"I didn't mean to startle you, my friend," Russell said. "I just wanted to make sure you were all right."

The man ran a bruised hand over his face. His knuckles were black and blue, his fingers covered with cuts that hadn't really been tended, but which were obviously healing.

Once the man's hand came down, though, his expression seemed calmer. Perhaps he too was a member of the repressed. Or perhaps, like Russell, simply someone who could set emotions aside when necessary.

"I'm all right," the man said.

"You didn't look all right," Russell said. He approached from the side, making sure the bench's ornate arm was between him and the man.

The man was wearing gray pants that were not tattered, a light green shirt that had no blood on it, and black military-issue boots that had a lot of wear.

"I am a good listener," Russell said, "if that's what you need."

The man's face relaxed into a near-smile. It was almost as if he couldn't quite bring himself to commit to a real smile.

"You ever have one of those days," the man asked, "where it didn't matter what you did? Nothing went right, and because nothing went right, nothing would go right again."

Days like that were why Russell dealt with families, not active military. The heartbreak he saw in those left behind was enough; the heartbreak of those still active was beyond him.

Too many choices in the field, too much death, too many unresolved crises.

So Russell did not answer the question, not directly.

Instead he walked around the man as if the man were a slightly feral animal that needed to be approached with caution.

"Who did you lose?" Russell asked.

The man made that half-smile again, only this time, it was filled with regret. He looked away, at the water, which was still sparkling, as if this conversation made it feel merry.

"Who didn't I lose?" the man asked.

"Today?" Russell asked, because if the loss had been recent, he might be able to put the man into one of his programs.

"This week, last month, two years ago," the man said. "It's never-ending." He rubbed that damaged hand on his pants legs. "Then they sent me here to relax. I have no idea how to relax. Relaxation won't help. People die because of relaxation, you know? Because they're not paying attention."

"But you heard me come," Russell said.

"When you'd already gotten too close." The man leaned forward and put his elbows on his thighs, hands dangling over his knees. "You ever ask why we're doing all of this?"

Every day, Russell thought, but knew that answer was too glib for this conversation.

"Yeah," he said flatly.

"I think it got lost," the man said. "They tell me there was a reason once, but now, we're just . . ." Then, that wary half-smile again. "You didn't come here for philosophy."

"I came here to see if you were all right," Russell said.

"No, of course I'm not all right," the man said. "How could I be? None of us are. They're breaking us all, one by one."

They. The elusive and non-specific *they*. Russell had used it a lot himself.

But what he didn't say, what he couldn't say, was that *they*—the elusive and non-specific *they*—were probably broken too. No one was going to come through these years unscathed.

He had long ago stopped hoping for wisdom from leaders and had simply accepted the need to get through each and every day, trying to do something good.

It sounded fatuous, even unspoken.

"What broke you today?" Russell asked, worried that the question was too specific for this conversation.

The man looked at him directly, as if seeing him for the first time. "Why do you care?"

"I . . ." Russell didn't want to say *It's my job*, because that sounded too callous. *It's my training* had the same problems. "I . . . I . . ." The truth, then. "I was actually worried you might be dead."

The man laughed. It was a real laugh, deep and powerful. Russell hadn't heard a laugh like that in years, not since Raymond died, maybe not for years before.

"Me, dead?" The man slowly eased into a chuckle. "Do you know how many times I've died?"

"No," Russell said, keeping his voice even. There was a fine line between compassion and condescension, and he was trying desperately to walk it. "I don't."

"Too many," the man said, the laughter gone from his voice. "Too damn many."

ME

NO ONE HAD EVER SAID that to me before. No one had ever answered the question *How did he die?* with a *He didn't.*

Jessica O'Shea didn't say any more. She sat on my nicest ratty couch, hands clasped in her lap, watching me with those auburn-brown eyes, the images of the man she loved cycling over the table, waiting for someone to make a choice.

I mentally reviewed our conversation. I had given her the standard disclaimers, but built into them was a caution. I had said *someone you lost*, not *someone who died*. I'd learned that the words *died* and *death* were trigger words, sending people into spasms of grief that I didn't really want to deal with.

"There are actual detectives in this city," I said. "They

find missing people—people whom we know are alive and functioning somewhere in this sector."

Her eyes narrowed, her mouth thinned. "I received a death notice," she said. "I don't believe it."

I let out a small breath, but did not close my own eyes in frustration, much as I wanted to do so. People who did not believe death notices had powerful minds and imaginations, so powerful, in fact, that they could convince themselves that they saw the dead walking the streets even when they had proof that the person was long gone.

Now I had to figure out how to get her out of my office —to fire the client, so to speak, before she had even officially hired me.

"Let me see the death notice." I'd gone through this sort of routine nearly a dozen times. It was not one that I liked. It was going to end in an angry outburst, one that might become physical.

I braced myself.

She reached into her small clutch, and removed one of the storage devices. It was tiny, more modern device than the handheld. It was the size of her thumb. It was not any kind of implant, that would require her to send something directly to me.

In that, we shared a kinship. I did not like any implants either. I didn't trust anyone else's information to seep into my body, sometimes in ways that I couldn't prevent.

"I can show it to you," she said tightly, "or I can send it to you."

"Show it to me, please," I said. My table would record it. I had dozens of death notices stored in my files, thanks to that table. I could tell which ones were valid at a glance.

She pressed the side of the device and a death notice floated above her hand. She had to hit the device again so that the notice faced me.

On one side was a military portrait of the man whose sleeping image I had seen. His face was pudgier than I expected, his eyes less wary than the eyes of most who had their images stored at the beginning of their careers.

Something was off about the image, something I didn't have time to analyze.

The notice had the proper dates, and an option to have it read to me. I could even choose what kind of voice, accent, and language I wanted to hear it in.

We have been requested to inform you, as the designated fiancé, *of the death of Keenan Izu. Keenan Izu died as a result of weapons fire in* **redacted**. *Images of the body, already identified by the officer in charge, can be provided upon request. Due to circumstances on the ground, his body is unavailable for return.*

Keenan Izu listed you as the recipient of his survivor benefits. To access them, contact . . .

I looked at the various contact points, which were often a way for scammers to hijack the information of the survivors. The contact points looked legitimate, even though I might test them later.

Depending on what happened next.

I did not comment on the validity of the death notif-ication. I'd learned to avoid that as well.

"Did you apply for the death benefits?" I asked, keeping my voice level.

"After I saw the images, yes," she said.

"You asked for his death images?" I asked. Most people did not.

"Yes."

"And you have those?" I asked.

Her lips curled. "They're fake."

I did not ask her how she knew that. I'd heard the same comment from many people when they saw the images. The images never looked like the deceased had looked in life. There was a lack, an emptiness, an unreality that was clear in person, but accented in imagery.

The dead never were their bodies. The bodies are clearly left behind, something humans had commented on since the beginning of time.

No amount of science, no amount of study, could tell us why. I always thought it was to make the transition between life and loss easier. We saw something that was missing—an animation, a guiding spirit.

And that something was not anything I discussed with my clients.

Ever.

"But do you have the images?" I asked.

"I don't carry them around with me," she said. "I told you. They're fake."

"I'd like to see them," I said.

"To see how crazy I am?" she snarled. There was the emotion—anger, and beneath it, something else. Denial, probably. I was making her confront something she didn't want to see.

I didn't respond to that. She grabbed her clutch again, and I thought she was going to put the little drive back inside it. She did do that, but then came out with another and tossed it at me.

I caught it with one hand, startled. People didn't usually toss storage devices at me.

"You can have it," she said with a bit too much anger. "I don't want to see them again. They're *fake*, but you're going to have to figure that out for yourself, aren't you?"

That was the conversation I had planned to have with her, all about bodies and how we see them and how they always looked fake.

I set the device on my side of the table, and resisted the urge to wipe my palms on my pants. One more question, and we would probably be done.

"If you think the images are fake," I said, "why did you apply for the benefits?"

She glared at me with a hatred I hadn't expected.

"He's alive, I'm telling you," she said with great fury.

She wasn't going to answer my question, at least not yet.

"What happened to him, then?" I asked. "If he didn't die."

I expected one of the plots from an entertainment: *Oh, he had been so badly injured, he didn't remember me. So when he came home, he didn't try to find me.*

Instead, she said, "At first, I thought he was in a coma somewhere, unconscious and warehoused. You know they do that, right? To the most seriously injured?"

I'd heard rumors since the start of the war about such things, bodies kept alive so that their organs could be farmed. But that made no sense, considering the hospitals could grow new organs that wouldn't be rejected.

None of the conspiracy theories made sense, but I'd learned long ago not to confront a conspiracy theorist.

"At first," I repeated. "But now?"

"I've seen him, I told you." She clutched her hands together in her lap, forming small fists. Her fury was becoming unnerving. "All over Naik. I have images."

"Of him," I said, my voice flat. "Recent ones?"

"Yes." She pulled a third device from the clutch. She set the clutch on the couch, and held the device toward me.

I wasn't taking that. I already had custody of the death images. I certainly didn't want these, at least not directly from her.

The other images were still scrolling around the hand-held, Keenan in various positions, standing, sitting, sleeping. She had taken a lot of images of Keenan when he wasn't looking.

"Show me," I said.

She lowered her lids, and finally shut off the handheld, which was good. If it was anything like the other ancient handhelds I'd seen, the more she pushed it, the more likely it was to fail.

She tucked the handheld in her clutch, set the clutch on her lap, and then squeezed the third device.

Blurry images, mostly three-dimensional, appeared above her hand, small images of a man, usually wearing a dark coat, usually turning away from her.

None of them seemed remarkable to me.

"Where were these taken?" I asked.

She was sitting rigidly, as if she didn't expect me to ask any questions at all.

"Mostly downtown," she said. "Near the underground transport."

The system that everyone used unless they walked.

"Did you see him at the same time every day?" I asked.

"No—yes," she said, seeming to calm down. Apparently, the questioning helped. "At first. But after about a week, I didn't see him anymore."

I wasn't sure how to take that information. Did that mean some man felt stalked by this woman and had changed his travel times? Or did it mean that she had seen different men and mistaken them for the same one?

"So you only saw him for a week?" I asked.

"At that particular time," she said slowly, as if I was dumb. "I saw him at other times later."

I would set that aside for a moment. This case—if it could fairly be called a case—was rapidly devolving into the delusions of one grief-stricken, lovesick person.

"In the same part of town?" I asked.

I didn't think her body could get more tense, but it did. She sat so rigidly, I could have broken her in half with a sharp whack to her arm.

"No." She spat that word out. "I'm crazy, right? Delusional?"

"I never used those words," I said.

"But you're thinking them," she said.

I sighed. Time to haul out the canned speech again.

"I don't think you're crazy," I said. "I think you believe you're seeing him. But you're in mourning. You—"

"You said you could help me," she said, her voice going up.

"I said my job is to shatter dreams." It was my turn to speak slowly. "I warned you about that."

"I don't dream about anything," she said.

"You dream that he's still alive, but part of you knows he's not. You received the death notice, requested the images, and after seeing them, asked for the death benefits. Answer me one question: did you start seeing him just after you asked for those benefits?"

She suddenly became very pale. I had touched a nerve, probably hitting the spot she'd been trying to conceal from herself for a long time.

I lowered my voice, made myself sound as gentle as I could. "Deep down," I said, "you know he's gone. But you feel guilty taking the death benefits. Because you need them?"

She started to answer, but I waved her off.

"Because you feel you don't deserve them, given that you weren't yet married? Maybe you just don't want him to be dead, and taking the benefits confirmed it for you, so you're making up these sightings so that he'll remain with you."

She stood slowly. "You're a bastard," she said.

"Sometimes," I said.

"You weren't ever going to take my case, were you?" she asked. "You don't ever take cases, do you?"

"I take them sometimes," I said. Which was true. When they interested me.

This one didn't, not really. It was too mundane.

Although something caught the back of my mind, worrying it.

"You're lying," she said.

"Actually, I'm not," I said. "How else do you think I can maintain this fine abode?"

She let out a half growl half shout. She was clearly so angry that words had failed her.

She stomped away from my little furniture grouping and headed to the door.

"I'm not going to recommend you to anyone," she said. "I'm going to tell people you refused to verify my death."

Her death. That wasn't what she meant. She meant the death she had brought to me, the one the government had already verified.

"For what it's worth," I said. "I really am sorry."

"You're a fucking bastard," she said, and let herself out.

I sat in the quiet for several minutes, breathing deeply and slowly, calming myself. I pretended to have no reaction to the emotions of my clients, real and potential, but I had a lot of reactions.

I just didn't let them show in real time.

I was going to have to make myself a nice dinner, take the evening off, watch an entertainment that had nothing to do with finding missing people, and maybe go to sleep early.

I'd have to figure out what kind of self-care would be the best, because this little meeting had shaken me more than I wanted it to.

She loved him. That was really clear. And now he was gone, and she was left with some money and a lot of questions that would never get answered.

Like so many of us.

It was a horrible place to be.

ME, BEFORE

THE FIRST DEATH notice I ever saw was for my father. I was sitting in the high school cafeteria, back in the days when they thought the war would never come to Vorless. Unimaginable now, decades later, but then, stated as a fact.

The cafeteria was as bland as the rest of the building. Most of the learning took place in our dormitories, using the devices embedded there. The instructors could track the work we did without ever having us show up in class. But we did show up because that was the only contact we had.

Besides, attendance was mandatory. We got quizzed verbally to make sure we were the ones actually doing the work.

And then some of us went to the cafeteria together for

companionship mostly, although there was little to discuss. We chose our food from a menu that appeared before us as we entered the room, then got the tray as we walked past what we called the tray dump, and headed to whatever table we were assigned.

Usually, if there was more than a handful of us, we swapped tables without permission of the system. Otherwise, we dragged our chairs back and sat in the aisles, trays on the table and food on our laps.

We felt at loose ends, because we knew we were biding time. Vorless was neutral, too far away from either side (back when there were only two) to be of value on the battlefield. Instead, Vorless had become a warehouse for people too young to go to war, too old to go to family, and too worthless to be cared about.

We weren't called refugees, because refugees had a specific legal meaning that we did not meet. Most of us had no legal designation. We were just left behind. We were from the area and we needed somewhere to go, and that somewhere was the dormitories attached to the high school.

It was pretty clear that we were just going through prescribed motions until we came of age. Then we would get our assignments and head out into the wider universe to participate in a war that no one entirely understood.

I remember the day the death notice arrived as vividly (maybe more vividly) than I remember yesterday. I had entered the cafeteria a little early because my class ended early. None of us (including the teacher) cared about the political structure of Vorless. We didn't even pay attention to the so-called diplomacy that happened here, except to avoid the areas where the diplomats met.

I crossed the threshold and my personalized menu popped up. I'd been thinking of a bowl of peanut soup because the day was dark and gloomy and peanut soup always made me smile.

Instead of seeing the usual menu, the notification screen covered everything, asking me if I wanted to see my news in private.

That was ironic: there was no private in the cafeteria. I'd have had to go back to my dorm room, which didn't even cross my mind. I'd gotten notifications before, mostly about where my parents were stationed or if they had been deployed.

There was nothing about this alert that seemed any different. I set it to show me the notification after I had gotten my food, and I got my peanut soup.

I got it, set the tray down on my designated table in the far corner of the room—a table I'd never sat at before, but one that cried out to have windows on the back wall. Of course, there were none. The windows had been subsumed when the war started, in case the nasty part of the war had ever come to Vorless—and I opened the actual notification.

It read:

We have been requested to inform you of the death of

David Turo. David Turo died in the battle of Chi'ray. He was in a manned vessel, shot out of orbit. There were no survivors. Due to the circumstances, his body is unavailable for return.

As David Turo's <u>only child</u> you are listed as the recipient of his survivor benefits. To access them, contact . . .

I stared at the notice and stared at it and stared at it, long enough for people to swirl around me, the cafeteria to fill and to empty, conversations to echo and fade.

Finally, one of the grief counselors came. She removed my peanut soup, even though I told her that I wanted to eat it (I didn't), and took me to her office where she helped me fill out the documentation.

As my father's only progeny, I had the option to stay out of battle and she urged me to sign that. It took me days to do so. Somehow I thought I had to avenge his death . . . except that I didn't believe in his death.

I looked up the Battle of Chi'ray. It was a space battle. Ships were obliterated, often with laser fire. The ship my father had been on hadn't been shot out of orbit; it had been destroyed while in orbit. Pieces burned up in the atmosphere instead of falling to the planet below.

They couldn't send him home because there was nothing left to send.

Or so they said. It was after reading that I realized he could still be alive. I decided that the military had no idea who was on that ship. He could have stayed planetside and when the ship was destroyed, let everyone think he was dead.

The grief counselor tried to talk me out of that idea, but it didn't work. Instead, I investigated. I dug and researched and learned how to track people in this sector.

I was on the road to becoming the expert I am now.

I searched for him, never found him, and knew, in my heart of hearts, that he was gone.

When my mother's death notice arrived six months later, I was prepared. I researched her death too, found nothing that suggested she survived. Her death meant I didn't have to join up at all, but I did.

The military investigative corp.

I learned how to find out everything there was about everything. I never went near a battle, but I had researched hundreds of them.

And through it all, I went through the same stages as my clients—the rage, the disbelief, the anger. The potent and imaginative denial. The final acceptance, the kind that made the universe a duller and unkinder place.

I did not have relationships so much as encounters. I saw no point, as long as the wars continued, in getting close to anyone.

The biggest triumph I had in those years—in most years—was teaching myself to eat peanut soup again.

Although it no longer makes me smile.

ME

I DIDN'T RELAX after all after Jessica O'Shea left. Instead, I did something I almost never do.

I remained on my ratty couch, and reviewed the file. Something about it haunted me, and I needed to know what that was before I filed it away.

I peered at the images, particularly the images she had taken of the man. His posture bothered me. He was always trying to hide his face from the lens or grab the device she was using to make an image of him. She only caught his full face when he was sleeping.

I pulled up the image that had accompanied the death notice—the enlistment image or recruitment image or whenever it had been taken. The image of a younger man, one who still had some kind of hope, one who hadn't lost touch with the lighter parts of the world.

My eye told me it was the same man, and so did my software. Oddly, though, the image attached to his death notice was older than the images of the sleeper. I had thought when she talked to me that she had said he was conscripted after they had met, or maybe she had just implied it. I would need to investigate that further.

At that moment, though, my issue was with the images, so I was going to examine those first.

I kept the sleeping image open as I scrolled through the ones she had taken recently, noting that most of them were near the transport stations. Reflexively, I started a list of which stations she had seen him at and when.

She never caught him face-on there either, but she didn't need to. If I could match the timestamps, I would be able to find him on the recordings Naik kept of people who were traveling through. I might even be able to access his identification, just using the image alone.

Before I did any of that, I stared at him. Did he look familiar because he had a strong athletic build like so many who had gone to war? Because his face was square and slightly in shadow? Because he wore dark clothing that accented his dark hair?

A hundred men looked just like that. They moved athletically because of their training. They seemed furtive because they'd been to war.

The transport pictures gave me no answers, nor did they quiet the unease I was feeling. Something was off about this person, and I had yet to identify what it was.

I did not like the fact, though, that he wanted to keep himself secret. I did not like the way he avoided every possible camera—from hers to the transport station's. The way he ducked his head, his quick movements, all designed to make an image or an impression blurry and difficult to reconstruct.

My heart was pounding and I tried not to think about Jessica O'Shea. If I had to backtrack, tell her that I had been wrong—well, that would be humiliating, but I would do so.

Although I would not do so yet.

I saved the death images for last. They were oddly tasteful, as the death images usually were. If the body was too destroyed, there would be images of the head only. If the face was destroyed, there'd be a profile.

There was always a DNA form along the side as well, as if to prove that the images were real.

Everyone—or at least everyone who worked in the notification business—knew that the images were there for the survivors. No one truly needed millions of gruesome images of the dead. Posterity only needed a few to capture the moment. The rest of the shots, well, they were there to prove to the survivors that their loved one was well and truly gone.

Unless that loved one had died as my father had—blown up with no trace.

Keenan Izu had died leaving a trace. The images were not three-dimensional. Mercifully, no one had sent a hologram. In three of the images, his body was twisted side-ways, the shot clearly taken while the body was still in rictus . . . or the wounds were so grievous that there was no straightening of the limbs.

Possible, if he had been severely burned.

If that was the case, I was glad not to see it.

But his face showed no sign of destruction, no burns, no battering. The lighting around it was dim, the back-ground clearly and obviously altered so that the location of the body was hidden. But the face was clear enough.

It had the pudgy cheeks of the enlistment photo, the solidity of the jaw that seemed unique to Keenan Izu. His hair was mostly gone, almost as if it had been wiped away in the same action that had taken out the background, and his lips were pursed.

His lips were pursed.

I let out a breath.

People's faces went lax in death. They did not show anger or remorse or sadness. If anyone saw such things on the face of a corpse, it was because that person *wanted* to see the emotion, that person read the lax facial muscles as something other than what they were.

His lips were pursed.

I looked at the two other images of the face, which were very similar. Then I called up the enlistment image.

Keenan Izu's lips were ever so slightly pursed, his cheeks pudgy. The sleeping man in the holo still floating over my table had a relaxed mouth that showed some faint lines around the corners. His cheekbones were visible, his cheeks actually hollow.

They're fake, Jessica O'Shea had said to me with great confidence.

I had ignored her, because she seemed delusional to me. But she had been right.

The images were fake, but they were government sanctioned. And I had a hunch I knew why.

ME, BEFORE

THE DATABASE before me was voluminous. I could get far enough in my searches to find the database, but I couldn't enter it, even with my high-end credentials.

It didn't stop me from trying, though, until one day, my superior officer came to the door of my office and leaned on it, arms crossed.

The office was barely big enough for both of us. I worked standing up most of the time, so that I could surround myself with two-dimensional representations of information, dozens, sometimes hundreds of documents, trailing off into the distance, seemingly going through the white walls, even though the walls had enough protection to prevent anyone else from seeing what I was doing.

That my boss had managed to open the door and to

watch me for a few minutes showed *her* security level, and her willingness to let me flounder.

"You're not going to get into that database," she said.

"Then get me in," I said. "My latest deceased has links to that database."

"I'm sure," she said. "Ignore them."

"And miss a family member?" I asked. "We need to make sure the survivor benefits go to the right place."

"They will," she said.

"You don't even know who I'm dealing with," I said.

"That's right," she said. "And it was meant to stay that way."

ME

CLOSED SYSTEMS IRRITATED ME. Government cover-ups irritated me more. Government cover-ups in the name of military security irritated me the most—but that was because I had tried and failed to get into the government's closed databases, and had gotten so frustrated that I actually broke through the first level of encryption.

There I had found my deceased—not everything, but enough to know that she had abandoned her identity to go deep undercover behind enemy lines. She had brought a lot of secrets to light before someone killed her—not in the way the government had said, but in a completely different way—and I couldn't see any of it.

Breaking into that system, and my obvious frustration at the levels of secrecy, got me another job offer. I could work for the closed system, making up identities and ensuring that the document trail that the deceased left behind got followed . . . or I could have an honorable discharge at full pension, so long as I never asked questions again.

I took the discharge. I took the pension. I thought I had stopped asking questions. I had taken what I had learned in that work and helped people who were seeing phantoms, people whose grief ate them alive, people who needed to see the future when all they could look at was the past.

I considered that to be helping people. I wasn't sure if that was exactly what I was doing, but it wasn't what the military had wanted me to do, and I had convinced myself that was enough.

I leaned back on my ratty couch, staring at the sleeping image of Keenan Izu. I had seen death images like the ones the government had made of him. They had taken his enlistment shot and made sure that everything looked real enough—although it hadn't convinced Jessica O'Shea, who remembered starving with him during the blockade of Saanu, remembered how he had lost those handsome, pudgy cheeks.

Although she had never really noticed that his enlistment image was wrong as well. If he had enlisted after the blockade, then his cheeks should have been hollow.

They were not.

I felt that itch in my fingers, the one that commanded me to investigate further. I knew how to do it. I just never had, not in this business. I had looked at death images, I had examined the images people sent of the possible phantom, I had even tracked down some phantoms. Only two had actually been playing dead.

The others were mistakes, phantoms so close that it was easy to see how someone could mistake them for the dead. Those phantoms were often relatives, siblings, twins or children of the deceased.

I'd tracked down only a handful, but a handful had been enough.

Oh, but the others I'd investigated, those had been in my military investigative job, and I had found anomalies, things that no one else was supposed to see, things that had leaked out of the closed databases, because leaving no trace was worse than leaving a false trace.

I didn't have to look this up. I had already told her he was dead. I was wrong, and she had known I was wrong. I owed her nothing.

But . . . I couldn't let this go.

I got up, shut everything down over the table, and went inside my back room. I had a gapped system, one that had no obvious ties to me, and that was the one I opened.

I sat in a tiny room that no one but me had ever been in and opened enlistment documents. I found Keenan Izu's quickly enough, then I grabbed the image, and scanned it, asking the system to find me all other versions of that exact same image.

It found seventeen. Two were death images that had somehow leaked. Fifteen were different enlistment forms from different parts of the sector. The basics remained similar—height and age (give or take a few years). I had a hunch the DNA profile would be as fake as the death images, but would be government sanctioned.

All of the enlistment records came up red. Inactive was yellow, since anyone who had enlisted previously (even me) could be called back if there was a terrible shortage of personnel.

Red inactive meant deceased. Truly inactive. Inaccessible. Never to return.

Except Keenan Izu had returned, over and over and over again, under different names, in different theaters, fighting different parts of the war.

What leaked of the death investigations was curious, though. The deaths were never quite in the same theater as Keenan's supposed service. If someone with the classifications that Keenan had—or whoever he was pretending to be—had truly died, it shouldn't have been in action.

It should have been one on one, killed by someone he betrayed.

Since he had betrayed almost everyone he ever met.

TERRILL

HE SHOULD HAVE LEFT the moment he saw her, sitting across the platform, legs tucked beneath the bench, hands clutching an old-fashioned screen. His Jessica loved old-fashioned devices, said they were better than modern devices, loved the way that they fritzed and fumbled, loved even more the digital works on them that couldn't be found anywhere else.

Some people actually clutched books, but she read on tablets rather than on a screen that only she could see. Said she didn't like the way that people stared before them, eyes moving, but unseeing. Said she actually liked being in the world around her and disappearing in a made-up world at the same time.

She wasn't the love of his life, not even close, but she had been important once, and they had spent two great years together. He'd helped her through the blockade of Saana, and she helped him remember his humanity each and every day.

The years had been unkind to her. Her mouth had grown pinched, her eyes lined. The pinching wasn't a surprise. She had disapproved of a lot when he was with her, and he had excused it.

There had been a lot to disapprove of.

There always was.

That afternoon, though, the first time he saw her, she looked up from her old-fashioned tablet, saw him, and a frown formed over her brows. He turned away quickly, altering his walk slightly—not a limp, because that would imply injury, but swaying his shoulders side to side and making sure his stride was too long.

He went up a level, hopped on a train he'd never ridden before, and got off on the first stop. It arrived in the darkness of one of the tiny stations built for neighborhoods, not a hub where anyone could catch any train to anywhere in the city.

The overhead lights in that station were old and the coverings yellowed, maybe never cleaned from the smoke that had inundated these places during the last of the fighting.

He caught his breath, his heart pounding, realizing he had never seen one of his formers in the wild before. Early on, he'd made the mistake of checking in on one of them —a woman that, even now, he couldn't get out of his mind

—and his superiors learned of it, although he never knew how.

He was transferred that very afternoon, halfway across the sector, and put into remedial training because he had violated one of the service's major rules.

It was there that he had come up with his scheme, and thought it odd that no one had ever challenged him on it. Odd that maybe no one had ever noticed.

It assuaged his conscience somewhat, although not completely.

Something in Jessica's eyes as she saw him one stop back bothered him. The confusion and surprise, mingled with hope.

He probably should go to his superior, but he liked being in Naik, liked the life he had built here. It was slower than his previous lives, but the level of fighting in the area was smaller and he had risen in the ranks.

What he did now, mostly, was share knowledge, sometimes in training, sometimes as a conduit for those who were actually working. He had done his time in the danger zones, and while Naik wasn't exactly safe, it was less dangerous than any place he had been in the past.

Because he could, he looked her up, found she had moved here long ago, and it was only luck or chance or sheer happenstance that they hadn't run into each other before. Naik wasn't small but like most cities, it had patterns. He saw a lot of the same people at the same time every day.

Still, he had to confirm to himself that he had seen Jessica. He went to the same platform two days later, saw the same woman reading on a tablet—or rather, pretending to read. Her head was bent but her eyes did not track words. Instead, they were gazing over the edge of the tablet, searching.

That should have been confirmation enough, but he had to push it. He always pushed edges—that was how he had his relationships in the first place. He needed the human contact, yes, but he had also found a way to flaunt the rules without ever getting in trouble.

After the first mistake, flaunting the rules had become his private specialty, something he did to keep his brain active on something other than the usually cold and often awful mission at hand.

He started for the train near her, one that was about to board. She did not look like a woman about to board anything, though, seated as she was on the bench, her body tense.

He threaded his way through a dozen people on the platform, peeking in and out of them deliberately like sunlight through thick clouds. He kept his gaze forward, but used his peripheral vision to keep an eye on her. He also used reflections on the shiny gray walls. She had been wearing just enough red—a scarf and the designs on the sleeves of her shirt—that he could make them into a pattern.

If the reflection had anything like that pattern, he figured it had to be her and he ducked away.

But when he finally turned around, he realized that the color pattern he had identified as her belonged to a younger woman, wearing a turtleneck and a coat with bright red sleeves.

Jessica was still sitting on her bench, clutching her tablet, but she was staring after him with an expression that was frightened, intrigued, appalled and sad all at the same time.

He ducked into the nearest train, like he had before, and got off on the third stop this time, another hub, and leaned against a dirty pillar in a brightly lit area, letting people flow around him like water in an underground river.

His formers had never found him before. He had been careful. He had avoided the places he had served and the places nearby, the ones that people in the vicinity often frequented.

He had been careful, and still . . .

The pillar was cold against his back and he knew when he pushed off of it, some of the age-old dirt would transfer to his clothing. He could avoid that station and that area at the same time of day, but he couldn't be careful everywhere in the city.

If he went to his superior, he would not finish his work here, nor would he be able to help the woman he currently lived with, a woman whose nerves were fraught from her own experiences earlier in the war.

Terrill had finally convinced her to get help, even though her arguments against it were good: *We've all gone through the same thing,* she had said. *What makes someone else's insights more valuable than my own?*

As a younger man, he would have said that the counsellors had specific training, that the training had given them insight, but now, he knew that all counsellors provided was an ear, someone to talk to when there was no one else.

He wanted her to form a relationship with someone other than him, and she was inching toward it, but she hadn't done it yet. If he left now, she probably never would.

He swallowed, willed his heart to stop racing, and watched the ebb and flow of people moving on with their lives, no matter what they were facing. He couldn't know and they wouldn't share, not right now or right here. They were in transition, one place to the next, not thinking about the way everything could change in an instant.

That had been the beauty of his system. He would get involved, then "enlist," then "be called up," and then leave. Only later would the death notice come, after the new life had been formed. Only then would the slight worry that he might never return become certainty, and with that certainty, there was a bit of financial comfort, a bit of hope for the future.

It was his way of asserting control over a life in which he had very little control.

He pushed off the pillar, thought about going home, decided that was too risky, and instead, got on a train he'd never ridden before, determined to get off in a place he hadn't seen.

He had to change his habits, and he had to do so now.

That much he could control . . . and so he would.

ME

FINDING KEENAN IZU was surprisingly easy. I did it in the space of an afternoon. I accessed the public records using a pass I had gotten from a friend, and downloaded video footage of the underground platforms around the time that Jessica O'Shea had captured her images of him.

He had seen her on the third day, gotten on a train he didn't normally take, and escaped. Then he went back, apparently to confirm that she *had* seen him, and that visit had left him shaken.

It had also convinced me that I had the right man.

It took a little more work to get his current name, and that was only because he was on the lease for the apartment he shared with yet another woman, a woman who looked like nothing like Jessica except around the eyes—

that hint of vulnerability, of nerves, of a panic that was so incredibly close to the surface.

I found him and I debated what to do. People like him weren't used to being found. Spies did not like to be spied upon, although it was hard to avoid in a city like Naik, that had been filled with those kinds of grubby exploits since the early days of the war.

I bumped into him—literally—on a sidewalk near his place, using my own ability to fade into the background to make myself unnoticeable to him until the very last minute.

I picked a spot near a specialty coffee shop he frequented. It had indoor tables, including one he favored that stayed slightly out of camera range—for public and private cameras alike. The shop had table service, which also kept him off cameras, and I wanted to take advantage of all of that.

I grabbed his arm as I bumped him, and said very softly, "I need to talk with you, Terrill," and then shep-herded him into that shop.

It was easier than I expected. He was taller than I was and more muscular. He didn't seem to be carrying any weapons, though, and he did not fight me or try to shake me off. I had a hunch he wouldn't. Why do anything in public that would call attention to himself and subject both of us to the gazes of people we didn't know?

He didn't ask who I was or what I wanted. I had a

sense that being shepherded by people he didn't know wasn't unusual for him.

He let me guide him inside, and didn't even try to break free once he was in a familiar place.

The coffee shop smelled of roasting beans and sugar with a hint of cardamon, the shop's rather disgusting specialty. I had scouted the area out before I executed this plan, and that included trying some of the beverages and becoming enough of a customer that I wouldn't look out of place.

I herded him to his table, but not in an obvious way. I just kept one hand on his arm, and my much-smaller body close to his. The shop was mostly empty. A man and a woman were having a whisper argument three tables from ours. A skinny person in a black hoodie was using the in-person order feature, talking to one of the specialty baristas as they did so.

A faint, flute-heavy melody floated over the room, ostensibly to soothe us all. I found music like that annoying at best, but then this wasn't my usual venue. I didn't like to have my beverage experience curated.

I guided him to his regular chair then sat in the one closest, stretching out my legs so that he would have to climb over me if he left.

The shop had on-table ordering, which we did. I ordered something without the offensive cardamon and with a little too much caffeine, and then I ordered his usual, which was the house special.

He didn't say a word, confirming through his behavior that he was the kind of man I thought he was, always running into people he didn't know who had important business with him. Rarely, though, would they come into his neighborhood. So he had to know that this was something else.

When I finished ordering, he murmured, "Impressive," but said nothing else. I had started this; we both knew I had to be the one to take the lead.

I slipped him my information on a disposable tablet, one that was built for short-term work. He had a way of looking at it that impressed me. He touched it, but glanced down without moving his head. He was able to watch me, watch the shop, watch the windows, watch everything, and give nothing away.

I needed him to know that I was, in Jessica O'Shea's words, a people verifier, not a licensed detective. I needed him to know that part of her still thought he was dead.

"Jessica O'Shea hired me," I said after a moment.

He didn't start, didn't change his posture. His gaze met mine, but there was no surprise in it. He had seen her, just like she had thought, just as it looked like on those surveillance vids, and he had tried to get away from her.

"I haven't told her anything," I said.

He made a soft acknowledgement. "You think there's money involved," he said, which wasn't quite an admission, but it was good enough.

"I know there's money involved," I said, deliberately

misunderstanding him. He wanted to know if I was going to extort him, which probably fit into his world. "She received your death benefits."

This time he did shift, a micromovement so small that most people would never have noticed. Then he made a broader movement, leaning back and around me.

I thought for a moment that he was going to try to leave, but he didn't. Instead he looked to the side.

The tray was on its way with our two beverages. He acted like he had been looking forward to his.

I wondered if that act was for the cameras or for me.

He took his cup, which was tall and thin, and had a lid, and set the other one in front of me. Mine was smaller, and had no lid. Clearly the system recognized his order and not mine.

My stomach flipped at the smell of cardamon floating out of his. I pushed my cup aside. Coffee did not sound appealing at the moment.

"It's not just her money, though, is it?" I said.

I pulled the tablet back and opened another screen. I shaded it so that no camera could pick up what was on it, nor could any passerby see it without peering at it directly.

He watched my movements, his large hand wrapped around the cup.

"I see maybe a dozen death benefits here," I said. "Going all the way back to a Katrina Klein—"

"What do you want?" His voice was low and menacing. This was the man who did clean-up for politicians, found out dirt on diplomats so that negotiations could fail, figured out how to sabotage small targets so that it would look like the other side had done so.

This was the man who had, in a very small way, prolonged the conflicts that we were all living through.

"You expect me to ask for money," I said.

He tilted his head, his eyes glittering with rage.

"And that would be unwise of me," I said, "because you're not doing any of this for you. You don't have money. You're on salary. All you have to do is tell one of your colleagues what I've found and that would be the end of me."

He grunted again, which surprised me. I expected him to deny it.

"You might do that anyway," I said. "Or, rather than meet up with Jessica O'Shea, put a stop to her as well."

"I don't—." The words snuck out of him before he could stop them. I *had* surprised him and thrown him off balance.

"I used to work in military investigations," I said. "I was trained to poke at anomalies. The government made a mistake with your death notification. I can explain that to you, if you like. It's probably worth changing. If I can find it, I'm sure someone else can as well."

His eyes were hooded. He picked up that disgusting coffee, sending yet another whiff of cardamon toward me, and took a sip, although I doubted he tasted it.

"I have a hunch I'm the only person who found

these," I said, "because no one else is looking. If they did, it would upend a dozen lives, maybe more. I'm pretty sure I didn't find everything on my first search here."

He set the cup down. Most people would see no expression his face at all, but I did. Those micromovements. He was furious.

"But," I said. "No one else is looking. I doubt anyone will."

"What," he said tightly, "do you want?"

I shrugged, going for nonchalance. I picked up my coffee and took a sip. It tasted burned, just like every other cup I'd ever had in this place. I had no idea what made it special. Maybe the other ingredients, which covered up the failure of the roast.

Then I set the cup down. It was harder to say what I wanted than I had thought it would be. No one spoke honestly anymore, at least not about emotion.

"I guess," I said, "I just wanted to acknowledge how much I admire what you're doing."

His mouth dropped open ever so slightly before he realized what had happened and closed it.

"Most of us," I continued, "we stumble through this nightmare. We leave the jobs we don't want, and we . . ." become people verifiers, which is a rather brutal way to exist, if you think about it. But I didn't say that.

He frowned, just a little.

"You," I said, "continue to do the work. And then you

find a way to neutralize it. You add what you can to another life. Try to improve the world you inhabited before you leave it. I have no idea what you call that—"

"A little bit of joy," he said.

That didn't sound right to me. There was no joy in pretending at death. But I didn't correct him. If that was what he thought, then so be it.

"All I'm trying to say," I said quietly, "is that I'm impressed."

I handed him the tablet, with all of the information on it. He took it without looking at it. Instead, he was watching me like he had never seen anyone like me before.

"You're going to want to destroy that," I said. "And, for the record, I told Jessica O'Shea that her Keenan had died. She took the benefits. She won't challenge that."

A tiny nod. That was all, before one more sip of his awful coffee.

"I think you should put in for a transfer, though," I said.

"It's not time yet," he said, and I knew he wasn't talking about time for him. There was, again, someone else.

"Be careful, then," I said, and stood. I picked up my cup and put it in a nearby disposal, before adding, "Thank you."

His frown grew deeper. "What did I do?" he asked.

"You reminded me that not everything in this universe is terrible," I said.

"A little bit of joy," he said.

"I wouldn't go that far," I said, and left.

ME, AFTER

I SURVIVED the days and weeks afterwards. I wasn't sure I would. I thought he might end me.

He did not.

I didn't see him again, but I did see Jessica O'Shea walking to her usual transit stop. So I hadn't jeopardized her either.

I had been worried.

I didn't talk to her. She didn't talk to me.

People keep coming to me for their phantoms. I dutifully look into some of the cases.

I still shatter dreams, although not as brutally.

I try to find a little spark in those moments, a way to let the person know that the death might have occurred, but there is often something left, something that makes them want to see the ghost of a loved one.

I am not a counselor. I don't try to be one.

But I am a man whose eyes were opened just a little, almost as if he had found a tiny bit of joy in all the darkness.

Almost as if he'd discovered how to look forward, instead of remaining stuck in his own past.

BUT WAIT, THERE'S MORE!

Want more masterful science fiction?

Go to wmgbooks.com!

Sign up for the Kristine Kathryn Rusch newsletter, and keep up with the latest news, releases and so much more—even the occasional giveaway.

To sign up go to kriswrites.com

Get the latest news and releases from all of WMG's authors and lines, including Kristine Grayson, Kris Nelscott, *Pulphouse Magazine,* and so much more…

To sign up, **go to wmgbooks.com.**

ABOUT THE AUTHOR
KRISTINE KATHRYN RUSCH

Kristine Kathryn Rusch sold more than 35 million books worldwide. She publishes bestselling science fiction and fantasy, award-winning mysteries, acclaimed mainstream fiction, controversial nonfiction, and the occasional romance.

Her novels made bestseller lists around the world and her short fiction appeared in more than twenty best-of-the-year collections. She won more than twenty-five awards for her fiction, including the Hugo, *Le Prix Imaginales*, the *Asimov's* Readers Choice award, and the *Ellery Queen Mystery Magazine* Readers Choice Award.

To find out more about her work, go to her website, kriswrites.com

facebook.com/kristinekathrynruschwriter

patreon.com/kristinekathrynrusch

bookbub.com/authors/kristine-kathryn-rusch